AMAZING RESCUE VEHICLES

HELICOPTERS

BY LORI DITTMER

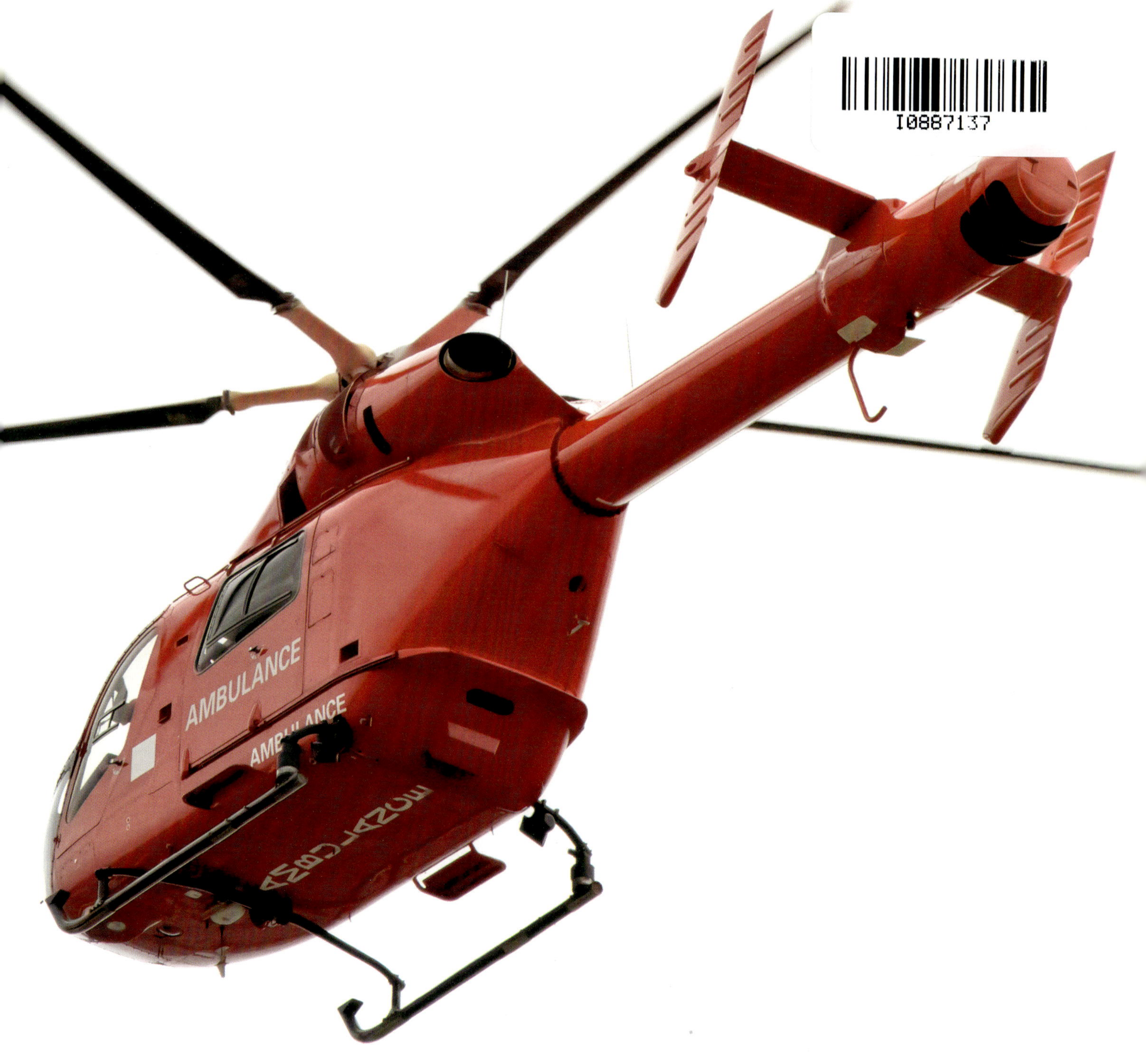

CREATIVE EDUCATION • CREATIVE PAPERBACKS

Published by Creative Education and Creative Paperbacks
P.O. Box 227, Mankato, Minnesota 56002
Creative Education and Creative Paperbacks are imprints of
The Creative Company
www.thecreativecompany.us

Design by The Design Lab
Production by Dana Cheit
Art direction by Rita Marshall
Printed in the United States of America

Photographs by Alamy (FORGET Patrick/SAGAPHOTO.COM, Lasse Kristensen, STOCKFOLIO®), Dreamstime (Laphon Pinta, Speedfighter17), Getty Images (dan_prat/E+), iStockphoto (Dan-Cardiff, dr3amer, PhilipGua, Spondylolithesis, subman), Shutterstock (Jaromir Chalabala, Alexander Cher, Digital Storm), U.S. Air Force

Library of Congress Cataloging-in-Publication Data
Names: Dittmer, Lori, author.
Title: Helicopters / Lori Dittmer.
Series: Amazing rescue vehicles.
Includes bibliographical references and index.
Summary: A basic exploration of the parts, equipment, and variations of helicopters, the flying rescue vehicles. Also included is a pictorial diagram of the important rescue vehicle and its equipment.
Identifiers: ISBN 978-1-64026-043-6 (hardcover) / ISBN 978-1-62832-631-4 (pbk) / ISBN 978-1-64000-159-6 (eBook)
This title has been submitted for CIP processing under LCCN 2018938944.

CCSS: RI.1.1, 2, 4, 5, 6, 7; RI.2.2, 5, 6, 7, 10; RI.3.1, 5, 7, 8; RF.1.1, 3, 4; RF.2.3, 4

First Edition HC 9 8 7 6 5 4 3 2 1
First Edition PBK 9 8 7 6 5 4 3 2 1

Table of Contents

Helicopters are flying vehicles. Some are used to rescue people. Early helicopters picked up wounded soldiers. Soon, helicopters became flying ambulances.

Early rescue helicopters were developed during World War II.

DANGER
RESCUE

RESCUE

Large Sea King rescue helicopters have been in use since 1978.

Speedy helicopters do not worry about traffic. They fly above roads. Where there is an **emergency**, they can arrive quickly.

emergency an unexpected, dangerous situation that requires immediate action

A harness can be used to lower a person to help others in need.

Spinning rotor blades lift the helicopter into the air. A tail rotor keeps it steady. Helicopters can **hover**. They lower a basket using a thick rope called a cable. They drop off supplies or pick up people.

hover to stay in one place in the air

Helicopters can land on mountainsides to help lost or injured climbers.

Helicopters do not need much room to land. They might touch down on a ship's deck—or on a hospital's rooftop! Some helicopters land on wheels. Others have tube-shaped **skids**. Special floats let helicopters land on water.

skids runners that allow an aircraft to land on snow or grass

Air ambulances take doctors to emergencies and patients to hospitals.

An air ambulance carries **patients**. These people cannot travel far on the ground. They need to reach a hospital quickly. Air ambulances have a **stretcher**, monitors, and other equipment inside.

patients people who are getting medical care

stretcher a cart with a bed used for moving patients

AMBULANCE

Helicopters can rescue people from mountains, water, and other places.

A pilot sits in the cockpit. This person flies the helicopter. Other people make up the crew. They are trained to help with different emergencies. **Paramedics**, firefighters, or rescue swimmers might be on the helicopter.

paramedics people who are trained to give emergency medical care

Some helicopters rush to wildfires. They stay above the flames. Then they dump water from baskets or tanks. They might spray foams and gels to slow down the fire. Helicopters can reach places that other rescue vehicles cannot.

Helicopters were first used to fight wildfires in 1947.

Search-and-rescue helicopters look for people who are lost or stuck. They can cover a large area. Bright searchlights help them work at night, too. They can fly over mountains. Or they can follow coastlines.

Paramedics may use a basket stretcher to keep a person still.

Amazing helicopters work with other rescue vehicles. Listen for the whir of helicopter blades near a hospital. The vehicle could be saving someone's life!

A rescue helicopter always has at least one person with medical training onboard.

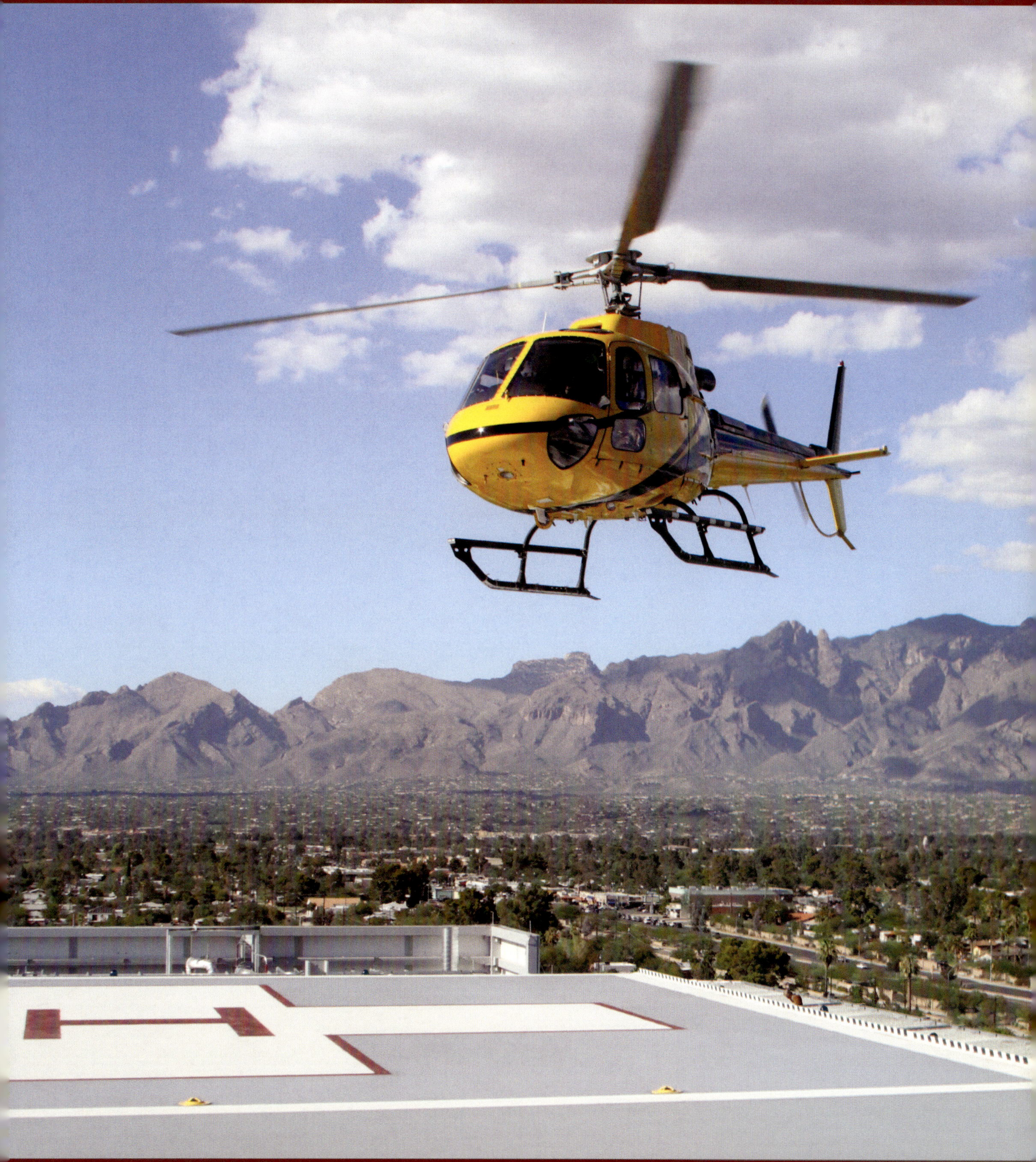

Helicopter Blueprint

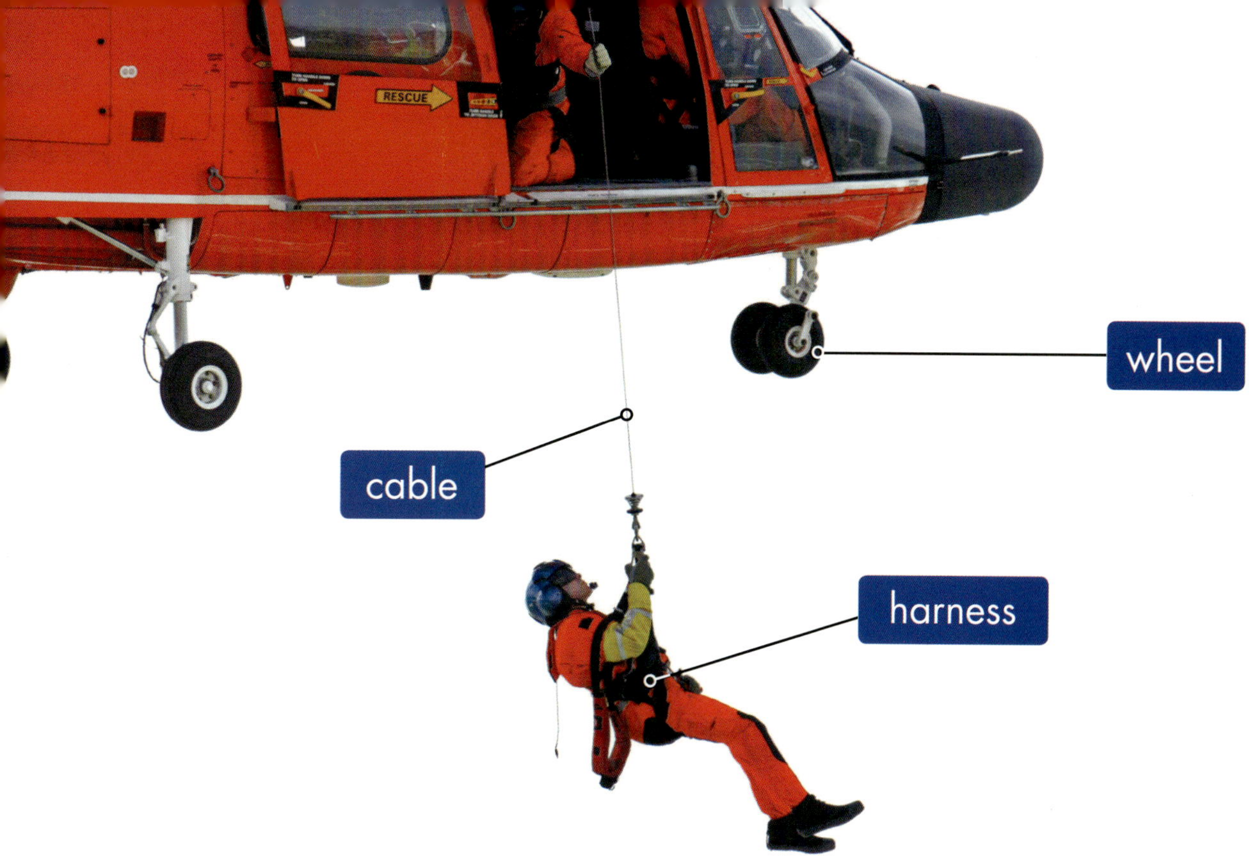
RESCUE
wheel
cable
harness

rotor blade
cockpit

Read More

Hanson, Anders. *Search & Rescue Tools*. Minneapolis: ABDO, 2014.

West, David. *Rescue Vehicles*. Mankato, Minn.: Smart Apple Media, 2015.

Websites

Gecko's Real Vehicles: Rescue Helicopters for Children
https://www.youtube.com/watch?v=a-FoFzXLMLs
Watch a video about a rescue helicopter and crew as they practice a rescue.

Westpac Lifesaver Rescue Helicopter Schools Program
https://www.westpacrescue.com.au/schools/schools-program-app/
Download a free app to play games and learn about helicopter rescue services.

Note: Every effort has been made to ensure that the websites listed above are suitable for children, that they have educational value, and that they contain no inappropriate material. However, because of the nature of the Internet, it is impossible to guarantee that these sites will remain active indefinitely or that their contents will not be altered.

Index